Macmillan Publishing Company
866 Third Avenue, New York, N.Y. 10022
Collier Macmillan Canada, Inc.
Produced for the publishers by
Sadie Fields Productions Ltd, London
Printed in Italy.
First American edition 1985

10 9 8 7 6 5 4 3 2 1

Library of Congress Cataloging in Publication Data

Krauze, Andrzej, date.
Christopher crocodile cooks a meal.
Summary: A crocodile prepares dinner for his cousins.
1. Children's stories, American. [1. Crocodiles – Fiction. 2. Cookery – Fiction] I. Title.
PZ7.K8757Ch 1985 [E] 84-12633
ISBN 0-02-750980-X

# CHRISTOPHER CROCODILE COOKS A MEAL

Andrzej Krauze

Macmillan Publishing Company
New York

My cousins are coming to dinner.
I'd better hurry.

I think I'll just open everything.

Fill the big pot with water.

Put it on the stove.

Plop goes the chicken.

I always feel sad when I cut
onions.

In go all the vegetables.

Stir up a little batter.

Do do be boop. Tra la la . . .

I make the best pancakes in town.

At least I usually do!

Hello, cousins. I'm so glad you've come.

Let's have some chicken soup.

And . . . oops . . . some nice hot pancakes.

Wash and dry all the dishes.

And now we can relax.

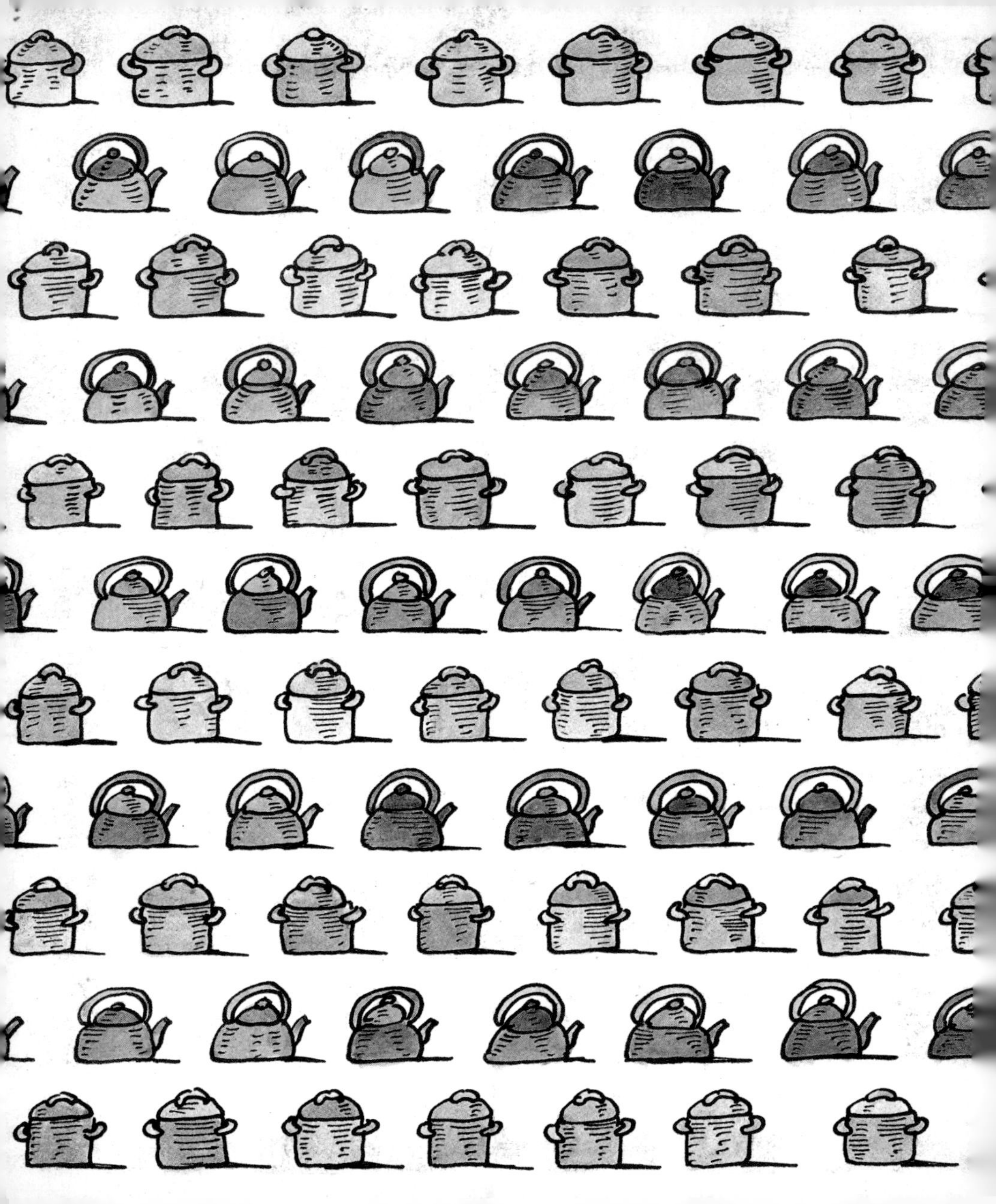